J PC
PIC
HIM

Himler, Ronald.

Six is so much less
than seven.

Six Is So Much Less Than Seven

RONALD HIMLER

Star Bright Books

New York

The name Star Bright Books and the logo are trademarks of Star Bright Books, Inc.
Published by Star Bright Books, Inc., New York.
Star Bright Books may be contacted at The Star Building, 42-26 28th Street, Suite 2C,
Long Island City, NY 11101, or visit www.starbrightbooks.com.
Printed in China   9   8   7   6   5   4   3   2   1

Library of Congress Cataloging-in-Publication Data

Himler, Ronald.
  Six is so much less than seven / Ronald Himler.
      p. cm.
Summary: After the death of one of his seven cats, an old man finds how
much he misses his cat as he goes about the activities of each day.
  ISBN 1-887734-91-0
  [1. Cats—Fiction. 2. Grief—Fiction.] I. Title.
  PZ7.H5684 Si 2002
  [E]—dc21
                              2002000294

to Scruffy

When waking in the morning,
six is so much less than seven.

When getting the milk,

When eating breakfast,

When cleaning the house,

When fixing the tractor,

When mowing the fields,

When painting the shed,

When taking a rest,

When going to get the mail,

When mending the fence,

When cleaning the barn,

When picking tomatoes,

When taking a walk,

But most of all, when visiting an old friend,

six is so much less than seven.